JAMES

PERCY

## MEET ALL THESE FRIENDS IN BUZZ BOOKS:

Thomas the Tank Engine
The Wind in the Willows
Skeleton Warriors
Fireman Sam
In My Pocket

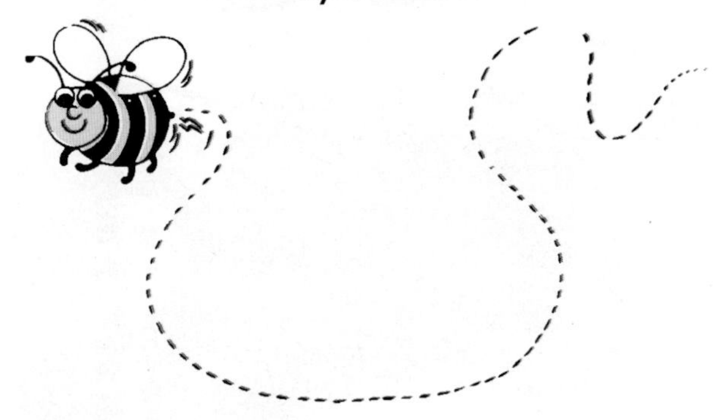

First published in Great Britain 1996
by Buzz Books
an imprint of Reed Children's Books
Michelin House, 81 Fulham Road, London SW3 6RB
and Auckland, Melbourne, Singapore and Toronto


Photographs by David Mitton and Terry Permane for Britt Allcroft's production of *Thomas the Tank Engine and Friends*

ISBN 1 85591 559 6

Printed in Italy by Olivotto

FOUR LITTLE ENGINES
STATION
buzz books

If you should visit a place that has a lake in the woods and a beautiful waterfall, then you may also find two busy little engines called Skarloey and Rheneas. The engines know everybody and everybody knows them.

There are two more engines – Sir Handel and Peter Sam. They used to be called Stuart and Falcon but they like their new names better.

The four little engines are happy on their line which is run by the Thin Controller.

One day, the Fat Controller sent Edward to the works to be mended. A big surprise awaited him.

"It's Skarloey. What's he doing here!?"

Edward knew all about Skarloey and Rheneas. He had brought passengers who wanted to travel up to the lake and the waterfall to meet the train.

Skarloey was pleased to see Edward.

"I've been sent here for a rest," he sighed. "I was put in this shed so that I could see everything and not be lonely. But I do miss Rheneas. He's going to be mended. I wish I could be mended too and pull coaches again."

Just then some workmen arrived.

"We're going to take you to the works now Edward. Come along."

"Goodbye, Skarloey. Your railway is a lovely line."

"Oh it is, it is. You've cheered me up Edward. Goodbye."

Meanwhile, Sir Handel was having trouble with some coaches.

He tried to be kind but the coaches didn't trust him. They were awkward and rude.

There was worse to come. Some sheep were grazing near the line. They were being careless and had strayed onto the track.

"He's bumped us," screamed the coaches. "Let's pay him out."

The coaches were so cross that they didn't mind what they did. They surged into Sir Handel, and pushed him off the rails.

No-one was hurt but Sir Handel limped sadly to the shed.

"No more work for you today," said his driver. "How are we going to pull the visitors' train without an engine?"

"What about me, Sir?" a voice piped up.

"Skarloey, can you do it?" asked Sir Handel's driver.

"I'll try," said the old engine.

Before long, his fire was alight and he started to build up steam again.

The coaches stood ready at the platform.

"I'm ashamed of you," scolded the old engine. "You might have hurt your passengers."

The coaches quivered. “We’re sorry, Skarloey.”

The guard blew the whistle and their journey began.

Skarloey remembered all the gates and stiles where he had to stop.

The sun shone and the rails were dry.
"This is lovely," sang Skarloey.

Presently, the line grew steep.

Skarloey fell short of steam and started to struggle.

“Take your time,” soothed his driver.

“It’ll be better downhill,” Skarloey said to himself.

But it wasn't. His springs were weak and the rail joints jarred his wheels.

"I feel all crooked," he complained.

"We'll need a bus now for our passengers," sighed the driver.

"No," pleaded Skarloey, "I'll get them to the station or burst."

James was waiting at the platform.

Clanging and clanking, Skarloey steamed in.

"I'll do it, I'll do it, I've done it!" he announced triumphantly.

James collected his passengers and respectfully puffed away. Everyone was pleased with Skarloey, but he was still worried.

"Old engines can't pull trains like the young ones can," he said.

“They can if they’re mended, Old Faithful,” smiled his driver. “And that’s what’s going to happen to you. You deserve it.”

THOMAS

EDWARD

GORDON